11-08

D0535871

REUBEN and the BALLOON

P. BUCKLEY MOSS, Artist
Story by MERLE GOOD

Good Books

Intercourse, PA 17534 • 800/762-7171
www.GoodBooks.com

REUBEN AND THE BALLOON
Text copyright © 2008 by Good Books, Intercourse, PA 17534
Art copyright © 2008 by P. Buckley Moss
Design by Cliff Snyder
International Standard Book Number: 978-1-56148-639-7
Library of Congress Catalog Card Number: 2008022266

Library of Congress Cataloging-in-Publication Data
Good, Merle, 1946-
   Reuben and the balloon / P. Buckley Moss, artist ; story by Merle Good.
       p. cm.
   Summary: Reuben loves watching hot air balloons as they fly over
his Amish family's farm, and one day he is offered the opportunity to
take a ride in one.
   ISBN 978-1-56148-639-7 (hardcover : alk. paper) [1. Hot air
balloons--Fiction. 2. Farm life--Fiction. 3. Amish--Fiction.] I. Moss,
P. Buckley (Pat Buckley), 1933- ill. II. Title.
   PZ7.G5998Rdm 2008
   [E]--dc22   2008022266

Reuben had seen balloons before. Big balloons.

Almost as big as the clouds. Slowly sailing silently across the sky.

Sometimes in the morning, just before breakfast, Reuben spotted a big balloon overhead, floating over the orchard. He liked to run out of the barn and watch it glide just above him. So, so close.

But his older sister Annie scolded him. "Come and feed the calves," she called. Almost as though she didn't see the big floating beauty.

One time last year, Reuben was riding in the buggy with his grandfather when, all at once, Dawdi said, "Let's see if we can beat that balloon!" And off they raced, trying to go faster than the pink and green balloon. And even though it looked

as though it hardly moved, the balloon was soon far ahead of them. Dawdi laughed as they turned the corner for home. "That balloon's a thing of wonder," he said.

One evening at chore time, Reuben watched a big purple and gold balloon drift over the neighbor's farm.

Suddenly it started to come down. Reuben ran up the
hill to watch. It landed in a field close to the farm where his
friends Sam and Ben lived.

Reuben was sure that the calves could wait a little. He saw his father by the silo and called to him, "I'm going to see the

balloon." Then he took off across the field toward that purple and gold balloon. Annie didn't understand about balloons.

Two people stood in the basket hanging below the balloon.

"They asked for some water to drink," Sam explained to Reuben. "Must be hot and dry up there," Ben added.

Mr. and Mrs. Johnson looked at each other and then at the three boys as they gulped the water Sam and Ben's father handed them. "Do you boys want to go for a short ride?" Reuben couldn't believe it. "That is, if you're not afraid!"

By now, Datt and Sadie and Barbie had come to see the balloon, too. Reuben looked at his father. Would he say "Yes"? He did. "Be careful," Datt said. Reuben felt a big smile spread across his face.

Mr. Johnson helped the three boys climb into the basket.

Mrs. Johnson pulled a cord, and there was a soft hissing sound. The flame shot up, blowing hot air into the big balloon.

The hot air filled the balloon and the basket lifted off the ground. Reuben grabbed on to the high side of the basket as they went up. He waved to Datt and his sisters on the ground below. They were getting smaller and smaller.

Tiny little buggies drove down the winding road beyond the creek, near the covered bridge. "Look how teeny they are,"

he pointed out to the twins. The hissing had stopped now, and everything was quiet. A dog barked far below.

There was almost no breeze, so the balloon barely moved.
Then Reuben saw his family's house and barn. How strange!

He had just been down there, and now he was up here.

Annie stood by the barn door, hands on her hips, looking up.

"Can we land at Reuben's place?" Sam asked Mr. Johnson.
And just like that, they started down. The house got bigger and

bigger as the balloon and basket came down. Reuben waved to
the horses in the meadow.

They landed with a bump. Mr. Johnson helped Reuben and
the twins swing up over the edge of the big basket. His sisters

came running. And the puppies, too. And down the hill by the barn, Dawdi stood watching with a big grin.

Reuben waved to Mr. and Mrs. Johnson as they lifted off the ground, the hot air hissing. "Maybe we'll see you again," they called down. The balloon went up and up, getting smaller against the sky. "They look so small up there," Ben said. It was true.

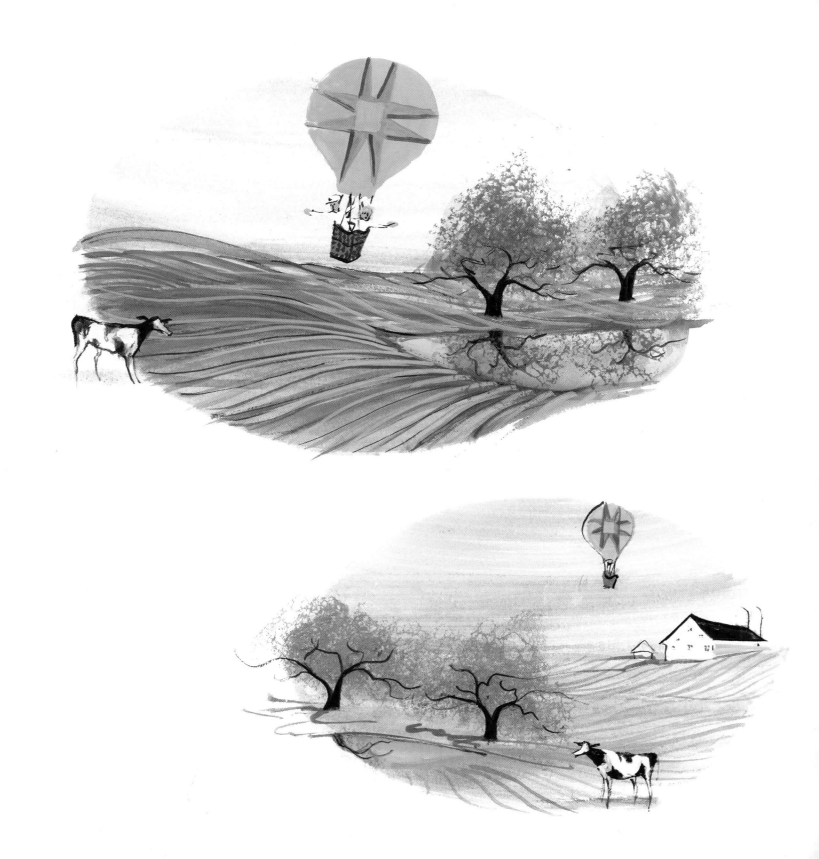

Reuben turned to see Annie by the barn door. "The calves are still hungry," she said. "You better hurry." Then she smiled. "I'd be scared up there, but you looked all happy like a pilot." Reuben just smiled and nodded to Dawdi.

Note

There are nearly 200,000 Old Order Amish persons, including children, living in 22 states and one province in North America. Reuben's family in this story is typical of the Amish in Lancaster County, Pennsylvania.

The religious beliefs of the Amish teach them to be cautious about many modern innovations, such as automobiles, electricity, telephones, television, and higher education. They observe that these modern things often fragment people's lives and relationships more than they fulfill them. For 300 years, Amish communities have sought a "separate way," emphasizing family, honesty, basic values, and faith.

For more information about the Amish, write to or visit The People's Place Book Shoppe, P.O. Box 419, Intercourse, PA 17534 (along Route 340), of which Merle Good and his wife Phyllis are Executive Directors.

About the Artist

P. Buckley Moss (Pat) first met the Amish in 1965 when she and her family moved to Waynesboro in the Shenandoah Valley of Virginia. Admiring the family values and work ethic of her new neighbors, Pat began to include the Amish in her paintings.

Many of her paintings and etchings of both the Amish and the Old Order Mennonites are displayed at the P. Buckley Moss Museum in Waynesboro, which is open to the public throughout the year. For more information, write to: The Director, P. Buckley Moss Museum, 150 P. Buckley Moss Drive, Waynesboro, VA 22980.

Moss and Good collaborated on the earlier classic children's books, *Reuben and the Fire, Reuben and the Blizzard,* and *Reuben and the Quilt.*

About the Author

Merle Good has written numerous books and articles about the Amish, including Op-Ed essays for *The New York Times* and the beautiful book *Who Are the Amish?* He and his wife, Phyllis, oversee a series of projects in publishing and the arts. Merle and Phyllis Good have also co-authored several books, including *20 Most Asked Questions About the Amish and Mennonites* and *Christmas Ideas for Families.* (Phyllis is *The New York Times* bestselling author of the *Fix-It and Forget-It* cookbook series.) They live in Lancaster, Pennsylvania, and are the parents of two adult daughters.